Bark at the Moon

A Selection of Poetry

B. D. Cotton

Contents

Bark At The Moon

They tell me that I am in here cos I, not very well,
If the medicine is working, I don't think I can tell,
I hope I ain't here long, cos I don't think it's fair
So, I sit on my bed and pull out my hair,
Talk to strange people that are not really there,
My wife keeps on phoning,
She says, "are you coming home soon?"
So, I say "to be honest,
I think i'll just stay here
And bark at the Moon."

The walls in my room are exceptionally white,
And the light in my room is exceptionally bright,
Sometimes I panic and start to self-harm,
But the Doctors soon cure that with a shot in the arm,
My neighbours are noisy and make such a racket,
But I can't bang on the walls because of my jacket,
I begged for the doctor to let me out soon.
But he just laughed, then said,
"I think I will leave you to bark at the Moon."

My wife doesn't come now, she corresponds by post,
Don't get many letters one a month at most,
It's gone on for so long now I don't think I can cope
So, I managed to get me a nice piece of rope,
The doctor came in and saw me hanging down,

Then turned to the nurse with an irritated frown
"Best get a knife and cut him down soon,
But I wish I could leave him to bark at the Moon."

Coudda Woulda Shoulda

This life of ours, there is only one A blink of
the eye and then it's gone,
They said I could be a contender for the prize,
I had a great big house a nice fast car
They said I had excellent prospects could go far,
I even had Trophy wife hanging off my arm,
We ate in the finest restaurants
drinking pink champagne,
With dubious women, some on the game,
All the gold and diamonds that money could buy
You know my friends I woulda had it all
Then I went and pissed it up the wall.

Now you ask me how it came to this
I've got no home and I stink of piss,
Well, I guess I never shoulda put that shit up my nose
Maybe never stepped on so many toes,
Now, I suppose I was never nice Made my bed,
Then paid the price, People tried to warn me,
But I never heard, If truth be known,
I guess I got what I deserved
People ask me where I go from here,
I don't have a future that much Is clear,

But I guess I only have myself to blame,

And if I ever got another chance You know
I think I would probably go and do the same again.

Hero

Oh, to be a Hero, may be a Master of Disguise,

Spider webs that shoot from my fingers

Or even X-ray eyes,

I could catch crooks by the bucketful

Put them all behind bars,

I could wear a fancy costume

Ride round in armoured cars,

But in truth, I am just a no one

Never going to amount too much,

Never going to be a Dirty Harry

Or a part of Starsky or Hutch,

No Superman or Batman fame

Is on the cards for me,

Not going to be hit by a special meteorite

It's a life of banality,

But I will be a hero someday

Life Is not all bad,

My Girlfriend 9 months Pregnant

I'm going to be a Dad.

Bet You Wish You Never Asked

You ask me how I am my dear, you know I'm glad you did,
Well someone gave my hiding place away
I think it was two fingers, Sid
So now I'm feeling anxious with the
cops right on my trail,
And if you ask about my complexion
I reckon I'm looking pretty pale,
I'm out of breath from running, and my legs are all a-quiver,
It's chucking down I'm soaking wet and
now I'm starting to shiver,
So now you know how I'm feeling, as I
stick this gun into your face
I'm kidnapping you and moving into your apartment,
Cos I need a new hiding place.

The Most Beautiful Woman In The World

In my humble opinion not that it counts for much
Is she the most beautiful? Maybe not as such,
She is certainly beautiful on the inside
She has a heart of gold,
Beautiful on the outside
Yes, truth must be told
Given me three children
She loves them, everyone,
Still got a twinkle in her eye
Always ready to have some fun,

She works sixteen hours a day
Yet does not have a job,
After twenty years of marriage
She still makes my heartthrob,
She tells me that she loves me
Each and every day

I still fancy her like crazy
It will always be that way,
I don't think I could carry on
If she was not here,
That she would stop loving me
Is my only fear,
Do you know? Who is this woman

Who brightens up my life?
Only one person it could be
Yes, that would be my wife.

New Beginnings

So, your bags are packed, you're sitting in the kitchen
Waiting for your ride,
Jesus Christ, you're such a coward, can't
even look me in the eye,
Where's your guilt? Where's your shame?
What am I going to say to the girls?
They are going to be gutted you son of a bitch
Though I know that you don't care,
There's the door off you run, go on
shack up with your tart
Don't you worry about me and the girls
I'm sure we will make a new start,
Don't come crawling back, when she throws you out
Don't you even dare,
We will have moved on. Got a new life
That old life will no longer be there,
I promised myself that I won't cry
At least not till you're out of the door,
God this life is full of shit
Surely there must be more
So, the door closes and I'm sat on my own
Wondering where I go from here
The only emotions I feel right now are
Emptiness, desperation, and fear,
Twenty-five years he has thrown away

He wanted to feel a bit younger

Well damn him, DAMN him, DAMN him,
We are coming out of this stronger...

These Are The Skeletons

These are the skeletons,
That are hiding in my closet
The more secrets that I keep,
The more that they deposit
They are building up for the big finale
The moment that I am caught,
When my secret comes out
The embarrassment I brought
I keep thinking I can get away with it
But it's only a matter of time
But although it is my secret
Is it really such a crime?
My life is all in tatters
My head is such a mess
Sometimes I just wish my wife would come home
And catch me wearing her dress.

Bugger The Vegans

Who wants to be a vegan living off nuts and rice?
I want to eat tasty food,
If it means taking an animal's life
Well bugger that, i'll pay the price
I want me a nice big slab of beef
Take off its horns and wipe its Arse
All this namby-pamby food
I tell you it's just a farce
How can you make a decent cake?
Without some eggs and butter
I can't look at a chocolate cake
Without my taste buds going all a flutter
I Want to savour a nice pork chop,
Accompanied by some kidney
A couple of sausages a pile of mash
That's what I want in me
All washed down with a pint or ten
And a couple of bottles of wine
If I offend a couple of Vegetarians.
Well, i'll tell you that's just fine.

My Poetry

I have always loved poetry, I do prefer to rhyme,
I wish I could write it every day,
But I don't have the time,
Don't get me wrong I have quite a collection,
Different topics and different styles,
I never always get it right the first time,
Sometimes it takes a while.
I could write about love, and philosophy,
Maybe, I could try to change the world,
But usually, it all falls on deaf ears,
And nobody ever heard,
But that does not bother me,
If I can write,
It gives me a bit of me-time,
When the kids are in bed at night,
I don't think I will ever get published,
Well not while I'm alive,
Maybe I will get it done posthumously,
But at least I can say I tried,
There again it's not about fame and glory
It's about doing something I enjoy,
And when I do eventually die the kids can say,
That's my dad's history.

It's Not Hell Is It

We have had the ups, we had our downs,

Worn our smile even our frowns,

Some days are sad, some are funny,

We have rowed about the kids, also money,

Been through it all, thick and thin,

But in the end, we always win,

We have had some problems as you can see,

But all in all, hell isn't a bad place to be

I Plus You Equal's Us

I want to make you happy,

I want to make you smile,

See us dancing in the moonlight

Laughing all the while,

I want to gaze into those emerald eyes,

Deep down to your soul,

I want to spend my life with you

Till we both grow old,

I want to have your children,

So, a family we can be,

I want to wake up every day,

See you lying next to me,

I want to hear you say you love me,

To want to see it in your eyes,

I want our life to be exciting,

Full of adventure and surprise,

But most of all I want to marry you,

See you all in white,

Spend the rest of my life just being with you,

Every day and every night.

Just One Day In This Life

Dad is on his way to work, He has his briefcase, and is wearing
a suit and tie,

Mum's a little pissed off, because he
never kissed her goodbye,

Dads works as an accountant, he
loves number crunching,

Mum's going to take the kids to school when
they've finished munching,

Dad gets to the office, Again. He has too much work.

He doesn't mind the office staff, But
the boss is such a jerk,

Why can't he win the lottery a million will do?

What the heck it's his fantasy, why not make it two,

Pay off what's owed on the house, maybe even retire

Spend the days just watching cricket, cosy
nights in front of the fire,

He glances at his secretary, fuck me, that girl is hot,

But would he take his chances, maybe, maybe not,

Sometimes he catches her watching him,
with those come to bed eyes,

But he knows that she's not interested if
she was, he'd be surprised

Mum's got the children into school, they're
the teacher's problem now,

She breathes a little sigh of relief,
subconsciously mops her brow,

She thinks about going to Mary's. For
some coffee and some pie,

But she's got her washing out .and doesn't
like the look of that sky
Dads too busy to go for lunch, So its
sandwiches at his desk,
He hasn't time to phone his wife, so
he sends her a little text,
Mum was going to have a sandwich
but puts away her plate
She's put on a couple of pounds and
wants to lose some weight,
Instead, she goes upstairs. She's got herself a toy
Brings herself to a grim climax. Not exactly exquisite joy
She felt the usual pangs of guilt but soon brushed
them aside,

She never did this often. Her little solo ride
She's always thought of herself as a one-trick pony. Missionary
style,
And they didn't get it much, Only once a while,
Occasionally she would treat him,
though she didn't like the taste,
Never has she swallowed, though
he jokes it's such a waste,
At 2.45 she picked the kids up, they were arguing again,
They fight like cat and dog every day
now, it really is a pain,
"Pack it in she says wait till your dad gets home," But she
knew he would not do anything,
When it came to the kids she was on her own,

While they were going home, she wonders
what to do for dinner,
The kids were playing espy, as always,
the eldest was the winner,
Dad got in at 6.15 he had been for a crafty pint.
He sensed a bit of an atmosphere. He hoped
there wasn't going to be a fight,
But instead, they talked about school, with
the usual how was your day,
After that was finished. There wasn't much to say,
Now its 7.30 and kids it's time for bed,
Dad gives them a piggyback and a swift kiss on the head,
Mum puts on the TV and dad gets himself a book,
She likes to watch the soaps. He just
takes the occasional look,
9.30 and its lights out, time to climb the stairs
He gets washed and cleans his teeth,
while she combs her hair
In bed, he's feeling horny, his heart beats a little faster
She just sighs and wants to say. Get
off me your fat bastard,
But she won't because she doesn't want an
argument so lets him carry on,
So closes her eyes and thinks of shopping,
jobs that need to be done,
Suddenly she starts thinking, of the nerdy
boy who lived next door,

Now he's just got back from Uni,
he's not nerdy anymore,

With his handsome features and
all-over homemade tan,
Of course, his bulging muscles. With
his shovels instead of hands,
Suddenly it's him. Who's raining kisses on her breasts
Rubbing his hands all over her body.
In a loving sweet caress
When he slides inside her. Yes, it's him again,
It takes her all her strength. Not to call out his name,
Dad, well he's thinking of his secretary, in
her little tight black skirt,
Her flowing golden hair, and her
white see-through shirt,
Her bright red ruby lipstick, on her luscious lips,
Picturing his hands on her naked, perfectly formed hips
He feels himself grow harder. As he imagines
her tongue inside his mouth,
Normally when he got in this position, his
dick usually flies on south.
Now its dads turn to feel guilty, he never
wanted to take this track,
But that doesn't stop him wishing, it was his secretaries nails
that were racking his back
This time they came together, with a shudder
a grunt and a then groan,
He kissed her and then rolled off her,
accompanied with little moan
As he rolled off her, she felt him dribble down her thigh
She should have felt exalted, but she
felt she wanted to cry,
Slowly he rolled over, and soon they were back-to-back,

He said babe I love you, she said I love you back,

They knew they were meant to say something, meaningful and
profound,

But neither wanted to start a fight, so they
never made a sound,

So instead of talking, they closed their eyes, and
they both feigned sleep,

Both assuming the conversation would probably keep

So, into the night they felt alone and never knew
about each other's sorrow,

This was one day in their life let's hope it's
a better one tomorrow.

Me Selfish No!

Married, you want to get married. Are
you having a laugh?
Sorry for sounding snappy? But why spoil what we have,
No that's never going to happen. I ain't moving in It's against
my religion, I ain't living in sin,
Of course, sex is different, that's just a bit of fun,
What you are you pulling a face for,
come on cheer up, Hun,
Hey, come on let me treat you, take you out for a meal,
But I am a little short on cash so it
must be a two for one deal,
I don't know why you're pulling a face
babe; you know that I'm poor,
Talking of which I don't get paid till
Friday will you lend me a score,
There you go with that face again, you know
I will never reach perfection,
I think you need something to cheer you up,
Let's go into the bedroom and i'll
give you a nice injection,
I can see you're getting annoyed, why
don't I pull down my zip,
You can let off a bit steam, give me a little lip,
Is there something up girl you had a bad day at work,
That boss of yours been giving you
stick i'll chin the little berk,
Look I think you need cheering up may
be we should have a threesome,

Before you dismiss it out of hand
think about it, it might be fun,
How about Ellie, your sexy blonde flat mate,
I'm sure she was giving me the come
on, last night when you were late,
We could set it up for next week
you could cook some food,
I could bring us a couple of bottles of
wine to get us in the mood,
Ow, what the hell was that for why did you slap my face?
What do you mean I'm selfish,
that I'm a bleeding disgrace?
You know what I'm fed up with your moaning
I don't need this shit in my life,
I'm getting my stuff together I'm going home to my wife.

Utopia

I have heard of a place called utopia
that's not too far away,
It only ever rains at night and the sun shines every day,
The streets are lined with magic trees, a
different fruit on every tree
The beaches are covered with grains of gold
and a beautiful deep blue sea,
They do not need money, because everybody shares,
Nobody hits their children because everybody cares
There are no such things as crimes here,
and prisons don't Exist,
No police or judge and jury, a peaceful place is this.
No religion and no governments thus no need for war,
As a bonus no salesmen knocking at your doors
No rapists or kiddie fiddlers what a lovely thought,
And after every evening meal a glass of vintage port,
But as with all perfection, comes a darker side,
Alas there is no football I can't watch my favourite side.

David And Oscar

It's now half-past seven and it's just passed Night, Night,
David and Oscar are wrapped up nice and tight,
David is seven he soon will be eight,
Oscar's a teddy bear, he is David's best mate,
Mum's just read them a story, now tiptoes out the room,
David's eyelids start to flutter, he will be fast asleep soon,
Now they are flying, they fly hand in hand,
So high in the sky as they soar over the land,
They soon see a Circus, with a tent white and red,
A ringmaster with a suit and top hat on his head,
Roll up he shouts, all walk this way,
It's all free to enter you don't have to pay,
We have lions and tigers, and friendly baboons,
Two dancing bears, and seals that play tunes,
The clowns are made up of elephants, and giraffes,
They get up to such antics your all sure to laugh,
They both got a ticket and entered the show
Just as the trapeze artists were taking a bow,
A hot dog man came and said they were free,
David had two and Oscar had three,
Then without warning, they were both up in the air,
And back into bed with seconds to spare,
Mum comes into the room as he gives a big stretch,
And a yawn
Time to get up son it's a beautiful morn,

She gives him a hug and a big sloppy kiss,

David gives her a big smile and said
What a great life is this

Just to Be with You

I believe it is my destiny just to be with you,
In everything I say, everything I do,
Every time I breathe it's you that I inhale
My life is full of colour when once was only pale,
Now I feel a winner, when once I could only fail,
I think that I am royalty a great and mighty King
Before I struggled to make a sound, now
all I want to do is sing,
Your eyes they shine like diamonds,
And I love that twinkle in your eye,
How I love the colour, A clear blue summer sky,
Your skin a bone white china. Smooth
and silky to the touch
Just to touch your lips with mine
Almost becomes too much,
Your radiance and beauty will never be surpassed,
My pulse is racing strongly My heart is beating fast,
I'm sure by now you realize I want this love to last,
The reason that I write these words, is
for me to win your heart,
Because you made me happy and brightened up my life
So, the only thing to say now Is will you be my wife

I Love This Poetry Lark

I love this poetry lark, but let's be
honest it's not rock and roll,
Won't be throwing no tvs. Out of hotel windows,
Or selling the devil my soul,
Yes, I love my poetry, but it won't bring me fame,
So, I won't bet getting caught out like Hugh
Grant with some bird on the game,
Poetry is such good fun but won't turn me into a fool
Won't find me like Keith Moon floating
face down in my nice new pool,
No, you won't find me on the TV or
the radio turning on the charm,
Won't be shooting no drugs with a needle in my arm,
Now you could say that I sound bitter
or got a case of sour grapes,
Why would I be jealous of getting in some scrapes,
The money and the groupies wanting
to shag me every night,
Hordes of screaming fans mobbing me on sight,
Could I be famous ever be that brittle?
Ask me if I'm jealous? Well maybe just a little............

One Sided Conversation

Well once again it's got to Sunday,
again you're not at home,
I'm supposed to have the kids today,
yet I'm stuck here all alone,
I don't know what you're playing
at, we decided this at court,
So, i'll have to go back home, throw
away the picnic that I brought,
I don't mind you threw me out the house,
moved me to this dingy flat,
Where the papers hanging of the wall
and there's no room to swing a cat,
I don't mind your shagging my best
mate we were over long ago
And the fact he's taking you for a
mug, I don't want to know,
He's been out of work for eight years
he's always in the boozer,
Never done a day's work in his
life, the guy is such a loser,
He's bummed my money, bummed my
fags, now he's bumming you,
Truth be known I'm not interested, I
don't care what you do,
But when it comes to seeing my children,
I'm putting my size ten's down
I love them dearly; you're not making me look a clown
You said it was for the best when you
said that we were through

I know it was for the best, it was the best for you
You promised you would never stop me seeing the kids,
Promised you wouldn't be that cruel.
And to think that I believed you, man I was such a fool
Soon changed your mind on that one. Now I
must get you to change it back,
I'm fed up with being Mr. Nice guy,
time for a different track,
So, I'm coming back next Sunday and if you let me down, i'll
make you pay,

And I don't mean threats of violence,
I don't work that way,
If you don't let me see my kids,
I'm gonna make you curse,
I'm gonna hit you where it hurts you
most, gonna hit your purse,
I won't pay any maintenance and i'll
let the mortgage slide,
Won't pay the credit cards either, there will
be nowhere to left hide,
Lover boy will show his true colours
he'll soon be on his way,
See how much you get on social,
beans on toast most every day
And do you think you'll get another fella,
Let's be honest the years have not been kind,
The fags and booze have taken their
toll, you know I'm right you'll find,
But all this can be avoided just let me see my kids,

My life won't be compromised
and yours won't hit the skids
And don't worry about the money I
won't kill the golden goose,
To be honest I'm just thankful that you cut me loose
And don't worry about me finding
another girlfriend or sexy wife,
I think you put me off relationships
for the rest of my bloody life,
I think I'd rather tie a paving stone round
my waist, jump into a river,
Or spend my life a hermit with my
TV football and my beer,
Oh yeah and two pieces of liver.

A Trip To The Park
1976

"Hey dad can we go to the park a quick
game of footie and a bit of a lark
We can go on the roundabout, swing on the swings,
Play stick in the mud, all sorts of things,
We could take us a picnic, and maybe a kite,
Stay till the day turns into the night,
Lease dad, please can we go,"
So off we went, me, dad, and kid sister in tow,
So, we had us a good time and got burnt in the sun,
I can't remember when I last had such fun.

Now

Well its 20 years later, look at me, see how i've grown,
I've got a wife and two kids a home of my own,
Last Sunday when I said, "let's go to the park,
For a quick game of footie and a bit of a lark,"
With a laugh and a grin, I said come on let's go,
It was me and my son and my daughter in tow,
But when we got to the pitch, "I said
we can't play on that grass,
Its covered in dog shit and look broken glass."
So, we gave that a miss and went to the swings,
Where we wanted to play hide go
seek and all sorts of things,
But someone had broken bottles all over the slide,
You can't go on that kids you'll ruin your hide,
Down by the roundabout my girl found a used syringe,

Who'd on earth would do that, they must be unhinged,
A strong smell of skunk comes wafting over the air,
It's coming from that group of lads stood over there,
Look at them kids, pretending to be men,
Shit look at that one there he's no more than ten,
I looked for a seat, but it was covered in shit,
Don't know if it was canine, but it sure
smelt a bit, So I decided,
Turned to the kids and said,
Les give this a miss and go to the pictures instead.

A Spaceman Came To Visit

A spaceman came to visit and his ship it filled the sky
People stood and pointed in wonder;
others started to cry,
The police quickly on the scene put
barricades round the ship
Looking very welcoming, with their
guns holstered on their hips,
Well a crowd soon gathered, it got
bigger through the day
The police told them to move along,
but everybody stayed,
The kids all got the day off, because all
the schools were closed
The city came to a standstill because the
traffic jamsblocked the roads,
The army soon came into the affray, they
brought their tanks and guns
Traders brought along their stalls, to sell
their coffee and buns
The media went into a frenzy, but
had nothing much to say,
The man on the TV said a statement
would be released later today
The president said "let's capture it
and see what makes it tick"
The prime minister just ran around in
circles, but he was always a prick
Priests from every religion, preached the end is nigh

That god would vent his wrath from
this invader from the skies
So now would be the time, repent
your sins, and save your soul
Embrace god and religion, that should be your goal
Peace and goodwill to all, well so the bible says
I can't see a lot of that, going round these days
Suddenly all around the world the
people started to unite
A refreshing change from them causing
wars and wanting to start a fight
Regardless of religion colour or even creed,
The people started talking because
they had a common need
From Africa to Britain America to Rome
the people shouted in one voice,
Fuck off you green bastard go home.

Happy Holiday Chocolate Monster

Her name was Maureen o Leary,
She could not get out of the house,
Her feeder was a man called Timmy,
He was as quiet as a mouse,
She had been bedridden for nearly three years now,
It took her an hour to raise even a smile,
Mealtimes were quite an achievement,
And usually took quite a while,
Breakfast was two packs of bacon,
A loaf of bread and two dozen eggs,
It was Timmy who did all the running,
No wonder he had such short stumpy legs
Lunchtime was three hours later,
Normally six fish and eight bags of chips,
Timmy would feed her so lovingly,
Then kiss the grease of her fat hairy lips.

Holidays were never an option
Let's be honest now, where would they go,
Timmy driving round in his camper van,
Maureen on a trailer in tow,
So, their holidays consisted of chocolate,
And they used quite a lot I can say,
A van brought it round in the morning,
Then she consumed it all through the day

For a treat Timmy would bathe her in chocolate,
Then lick it all off her skin, Paying particular attention
To the pool that formed in her chin,
This went on for some time
Till her heart gave up from the strain,
They tried but they could not budge her,
So, she was melted and poured down the drain

A Christmas Ditty

He's on his way he will soon be here
Once again, it's that time of year,
The kids are getting excited, Parents are getting stressed
The elves are wrapping presents Santa's getting dressed
The trimmings are up It's starting to snow
The lights are on It's all a glow
I'm hoping for a kiss under the mistletoe.

It's Christmas Time Again

Footsteps spoil the virgin snow,

The Christmas lights are all on show,

Santa's coming, he will be here soon,

And the kids wait nervously in their rooms

Ears primed for the sound of bells,

This waiting lark sure is hell

Dads are scurrying round,

Working hard not making a sound,

Wrapping presents, and putting up stockings

Wondering what they are getting from the in-laws

No doubt something shocking,

Christmas dinner with all the trimmings

Off to church to hear carol singing,

A couple of beers maybe some wine

Glass of red for me that's just fine

After all its just once a year

So, let's forget all our worries

Have some festive cheer.

Missing You At Christmas

Missing you at Christmas
The snow is falling, Angels singing
Kids are wondering what Santa's bringing
Yes, my friends its Christmas time,
Cold nights by the fire with warm mulled wine,
Tinsel sparkles in the Christmas lights,
The streets outside are nice and bright,
I have always loved this time of year
But that's all changed now you're not here
Is fade to grey memories of another day,
I suppose I have become a modern Scrooge
Miserly mean and downright rude
With you so far in the distance really hurt,
Knowing you with him just makes it worse,
I have no presents or even tree
All I want is you here with me,

Stood Up Again

I am in the diner all alone Are you out, or sat at home?

Yet again you let me down Another smile
turns to a frown

You do this to me all the time

It's not funny it's a god-damn crime

Being pretty ain't no excuse

I have said this before but it's no use

Another drink and your still not here

You're not coming this much is clear

I ring your phone but there's no reply

I want to die I give up hope and get the bill

I won't fall for this again

But then again, I know I will

This Life Of Ours

She wonders where she goes from here.

Feels like she's carrying a cross on her back,

Her Mother just wants to help her

But Dad says she isn't coming back

Johnny is still in the pub he says he don't give a fuck

She's homeless and got no money, really
that just sums up her luck

She walks to the park for some shelter,
almost like living a dream

Outside she's calm and collected but inside
she just wants to scream,

And the clowns go by in their thousands, but
she knows they are not clowns at all,

Just young kids with great expectations Who
are heading for a fucking great fall.

The Americans are still overeating, And
Disney has moved into France,

The British are no longer English, to
be honest we haven't a chance

All the girls just want to be like, Jordan, Big
Brother is still watching you

But the program we should all be watching
Is Lionel on give us a clue

In Britain the dads are all alcoholics, the
kids are all smoking skunk

All the mums are all going to Iceland, but we
all know they are just buying junk

The rats are moving to London Expenses
are much better there

They are supposed to putting the great back in to Britain
But to be honest they don't really care
Millions of people are starving, dying at the drop of a hat
It gets mentioned occasionally on twitter,
while people are having a chat,
The Phoenix has been sent to take pictures,
as we try to conquer the Stars
Trying to answer that question Do you think
there is life on mars?

Sink The Pink

You can lead that girl to water, but you
can't make her drink

But you can get her drunk with a bottle of wine

And get to sink the pink So, go and get your woman,

Let the good times roll,

Put your foot down sink that pink

Let her know who's in control,

Take her to a pub called the shaking hand

It's got a forty-two-decibel rocking band,

I heard the music is good

I heard the music is loud, what you are
waiting for go join that crowd

Sink the pink then brag to your mates

Sink the pink then open them gates

Buy a lager, buy a bitter, snort a line be a right big hitter

Sink the pink till you catch a fever

Go with the certs get rid of the teasers,

Sink the pink, sink the pink Pay that
fiddle till your fingers Stink,

Sink the pink sink the pink If she won't come
quietly ply that girl with drink

Hit that herd leave no survivors

Get in that car you're a nominated driver

Hit them bars let down your hair

Tell her you're going heaven want to take her there

Say what you like whatever you think Do what you need to
just sink that pink

Sink the pink sink that pink
Do what you need just sink that pink

Benefit Child

The fun we had conceiving you,

Thinking about the benefits we would get,

A council house, and free milk

This would be the best time yet,

Then I went into labour and I swore never again

Twenty-- four hours of agony never
been in so much pain,

Then the money started flowing in, all of that forgotten,

Never had so much bleeding cash, well we
spoilt ourselves rotten

Then you became a burden, wanting some of our time,

We were always too busy drinking our beer and wine,

So, we got you r special toy,

A taser for when you're a naughty boy

You can stay in your room all the time

If you make a noise, I can give you a zap,

While I drink my wine

I Am Scared

My body is trembling,
And I am bathed in sweat
My heart feels like it's going to explode
My house has been invaded as I was doing the pots
Listening to Depeche mode,
I Want to scream but I can't make a sound,
Need to hide, go to ground,
I can't move
Or they will know I am here,
They are going to pounce when they smell my fear,
I hate being a coward, with this streak down my back,
Wanting to run when I should really attack,
I know I should repel these invaders
right out of my house,
Is it my fault, my fear of a mouse?

I Will Never Learn

I have done it again, I am a fool to myself,
I must be out of my mind,
Covered in love bites, I look a mess,
When I am drunk, I must think she is blind,
Oh, that's just great, here she is now Why
did I give her a key?
Should I stay here and face her,
Or do I head for the back door and flee,
I could slip on the latch and pretend I am asleep,
But she would most likely kick down the door
Why can't I be faithful, pleased with my lot
But I am greedy and always want more,
I hear the key in the door, and I am starting to sweat,
She is going to rip off my head,

Suddenly, deviously, I think of a plan
If I don't pull this off, I am dead
So, I creep upstairs, and rip of my clothes
Wrap myself up in my bed
Hoping and praying that this will work
Pull the covers right over my head
Just made it in time as I hear the door close,
I quake as she calls out my name,
The adrenalin flows and my heart skips a beat
But surly that's part of the game,
She enters the room, and she turns on the light
"Baby you should be at work",

I said, "turn out the light I have a migraine
God my head how it hurts,"
"Oh, poor baby what can I do,
Is there some way I can help ease your pain?"
"No if you just leave me be a couple of days
Compared to others, I have had this is tame,
I have taken my tablets and just need some sleep
Just talking to you makes it worse,
So, it would be best for us both
If you would just make yourself scarce,
I will give you a ring in a few days
I will take you out somewhere nice,"
"Ok sweetheart i'll see myself out
Can I at least have a kiss?"

"I said it really hurts when I move my head
Do you mind if I give it a miss?"
"Ok but you take good care, get plenty of sleep
Give me a ring later on,"
Feeling pleased with myself, I heard her go out,
Chuffed to bits she had gone,
I gave ten minutes, then thought a nice cup of tea,
Time for a treat for little old me
Went down the stairs with a skip and a hop
Got to the kitchen suddenly stopped
There she was sat with hate in her eyes
I could not move I was caught by surprise,
Then she stood up and gave me a slap to my face,
Then screamed "you're a moron,

Why do I have such bad taste?"
I hate you Bastard, and I hope that hurt
Then she stormed off with a swish of her skirt,
I could not reply I was consumed with guilt or pain
Then she stormed out of the house and I never saw her again.

Call Me

My heart is heavy, and my soul is dark
I need to light my flame with a tiny spark,
A glimmer of love, a slim ray of hope,
Something tangible to help me cope
I never had much luck, when it comes down to love,
No divine inspiration from God up above,
No arrow from cupid in my broken heart
I always seem to stumble when I make such a great start
Often, I wonder, maybe it's me
But I when I look in the mirror Nothing wrong, I can see
So, I trudge through my day Paint on a smile,
I know I will find love, but it may take a while,
So, if your lonely out there, Give me a call
Post it on Facebook, And I will write on your wall

Friday Night Mayhem

Friday night lets go out and have a good time
Get us couple of wraps, have us a line
Lay into the tequila's a half a dozen slammer's
Get into a fight because I got fists like hammers
Pour myself in gone half past one
God she's still up what does she want?
Where have you been look at the time
You do it every weekend your way out of line
Shut your moaning mouth i've been working all day
Get yourself to bed I don't want to hear what you say
But still she's going on, she's getting right on my tits
I don't need this shit my heads is in bits
Won't get out my head wagging her finger in my face
Don't she know who I am let's put this bitch in her place
So, I grabbed her by the throat until she turned blue
Threw her on the floor what else would I do
She will be fine in morning I'm going to my bed
Get myself some sleep and rest my aching head.

First Date

I just had a bath, put on my suit,
I am wearing my best Calvin Klein,
Armed myself with a single red rose,
And a nice bottle of wine,
We have been texting and flirting now
for quite some time,
So, I asked her out, now it is my time to shine,
I got to the restaurant a complete bag of nerves
Wondering if she would show,
I ordered a drink then chewed my nails
When I saw her, she positively glowed?
We went to the table I felt so proud
As every head turned our way,
As I sat her down, I Just hoped
I could find something to say,
We ordered a drink, and we talked for awhile
Ordered our meal, Fell in love with her smile,
Everything going to plan,
Hoping and praying by the time we had finished
This lady would have a new man,

The food was perfection and so was she,
I could not believe she was sat here with me,
We stuttered and stumbled, made each other laugh,
When it came to the bill, I prayed I had enough cash,
I ordered a taxi then shook her hand
I'll be Honest that's not what I had planned

But my head was all in a swirl
Deep down in my heart I knew,
She was not that type of girl
So, I waved her goodbye said I will see you soon
And I skipped down that street
Totally over the moon

Scent On A Pillow

There is always something of you lingering,
A memory or a sound,
A photograph, discarded toy
Just left lying around
Every time I close my eyes
I see your smiling face,
That you left so early,
Leaves my heart with an empty space,
I try not to be bitter,
But sometimes it's just too hard
When I am on my own
I slip into your room
Sit and cry for hours
Wondering why you left so soon
I sit and hug your pillow
Breathe your soap and strawberry shampoo
It brings me back a little peace,
But it really isn't you.

The Future

Where will we be many years from now,
Wondering when, wondering how,
Clinging on desperately to our teeth and hair,
Hoping our family will still be there
Will they still visit us every day?
Or will they up sticks and just move away
What about the grand kids?
Will they grow tall and strong?
Or will they just stutter and judder along?
And what about us, how will we fare
I don't think I could cope if you were not there
Here's to anniversaries' silver, ruby and sapphire
Even then you will still light my fire
I won't be as nimble or quick on my feet,
But I will still make you happy, keeping you sweet,
Still madly in love after all these years
We have had good times and plenty of tears,
But most of all we still have each other
Husband and wife, friend and lover.

How A Dog Says Sorry

Don't look at me like that,

I was only trying to help

Trying to get your attention,

But you never heard me yelp

I gave a bark, stop right there

He was having none of that,

So, I flew into action

To catch Next's doors cat

As he ran into the house

I almost caught him with my paw,

But there must have been a gust of wind

Because it slammed the door

Now I was going very fast

It caught me on the hop

In fact, I was going much too fast

I am afraid I could not stop,

Now I know that you are angry

And you're going to scream and shout

But seems like I am stuck here

Please could you help me out

Just An Ordinary Bloke

She said she could not see our love working,

So, I took away her eyes,

She said she was not happy,

So, I painted on a smile,

She said I held her back,

So, I tied her to an oak,

I don't know why this happens,

I am just an ordinary bloke,

There is only one loser here,

And that loser is me,

When I get home,

Who's going to cook my tea,

It Will All Blow Over

Take a tip from me don't you give up hope,
You will get no release from the end of a rope,
Paint on a smile, a cheeky grin,
If anyone comes knocking then let them in,
You can't carry these burdens all on your own
Why spend your life just sat all alone,
Don't bury yourself in worry and strife
Don't lose yourself in this graveyard of life,
Here is a way to escape when you embrace hope,
Throw away that piece of rope,
Take my hand and together we'll survive,
And we will keep our dreams and hopes alive.

Nope I Ain't Buying That

I am on my knees but i ain't praying,
I am burying my head in the sand,
You have this world, this universe,
Right in the palm of your hand,
Preachers of every culture
Bow to your every whim,
Forcing us to listen to their sermons
Trying to make us sing every hymn
But to me it falls on deaf ears
I can't listen to a word they spout,
When it comes to all of their lectures
I say for pities sake please leave it out,

Now I don't want to seem defiant
Because I do think of you every day,
But because your such an under achiever,
I just can't believe a word that you say
You made promises of peace on this planet
And that the meek shall inherit the earth,
The fact that poor Jesus died for us
Has been forced into me since birth

Well now it the 21st century

Where the hell have you been?
I have heard enough of this bull shit
It might of well of just been a dream.

Walk In Their Shoes A While

Life's too short for bearing grudges
Little whispers, secret nudges,
Don't tell tales or tittle-tattle,
Spit out your dummy,
Throw out your rattle,
It's time for us all to change our ways
Smiley faces and happy days
Let's be nice make people smile
Show your friends you have class and style,
We don't know these people that we scorn
Not know the lives to which they were born
Let's give these people love and compassion
Bring back kindness back into fashion

Free Write

What shall I do what path shall I take;
I have a job in hand a decision to make,
Do I write about football a war or a rose?
Should it be a story, or should it be prose?
Maybe I should write about murder, a hideous crime
Oh, what the hell I will just write it in rhyme,
It's what I am used to so why change my style?
This is quite a good challenge and may take a while,
But I am ready and I do like a fight
I may even keep writing into the night,
But that may get boring and may lose me points,
And I have to consider my poor aching joints,
So i shall just ramble on till there is no more to say
When the kids come in ask Dad can
you come out to play,
So, into the garden for a quick game of footie
Then let my daughter paint my face so, I end up
quite a cutie.

Dust Into The Wind

All the dreams of peace on Earth,
Roll away like dust into the wind,
All the lies and hatred, live in the courts
Where the judges have sinned,
In the politician's pockets
Who's sweaty hands they thrust,
Live a life of Luxury, Envy Greed and Lust,
In a World that thrives on Corruption,
Hunger, Hypocrisy, and War,
I sometime find myself praying To a God that I abhor,
Please come back and save us But I know you never will,
So, we cover our ears to drown the sounds of sorrow
Yet we hear it still
The masses are unhappy Angry voices fill the air,
Politicians make empty promises
But we know that they don't care,
All these empty promises from These Liars
who have Sinned
Disappear into nothingness
To roll away like dust into the wind

An Empty Space Without You

Blank, dark, an empty space
That's how I feel till I see your face
Then my whole-body tingles And I feel so alive,
Without you I'm empty close to you I thrive,
The days before I met you My life was just a blur
I wandered this world aimlessly
Lonely without a care,
I'm so happy that I met you
Glad you let me into your life,
Now you see me down on my knees
Begging you to be my wife?
Now my heart is soaring,
You wept as you said yes,
I put the ring upon your finger,
I feel like i've been blessed,
I will never ever hurt you,
Won't ever let you down,
With you I am completed,
No longer a lonely Clown,

The Wedding

It would be soon time for the wedding,

And he knew where it was heading,

She said I will be your wife,

For the rest of my natural life

So, for the insurance

He bashed her head in.

No Turning Back

He says its only because I care for you,
As he lays her clothes out on their bed ,
I only want to teach you,
As he slaps her round the head,
Why do you need your passport?
You're not going anywhere
You don't need any friends
Because I will always be there,
I will do the shopping
There's no need for you to go out
And if you keep on whining
I will give you another clout
And every day she dies just a little bit more
Her ego and her pride
Just discarded on the floor
No one left to turn to,
He's made her break all ties,
When she looks into the mirror
All she see are lifeless eyes
A life that's going nowhere
Except maybe to hell,
Yet when she finally sees someone from the past
She says that all is well,

Never has she been so scared
Now all she does is wrong
Oh yes he can be good

But it never lasts for long
Every time he moves
She braces herself for another smack
How sorry is she now
That she can't turn time back
She does not understand how she can love him,
Because it must be a sin,
But every time she kicks him out
He always worms his way back in
And how she hates herself
For being so damn weak,
Sometimes she's so afraid of him
That she can hardly speak
But she knows she will never leave him
Now she's caught inside his trap,
Even if she wanted to
She knows, there's no turning back

Paradise

She took me down to paradise,
In fact she blew my mind
She made me come so many times
I thought i might go blind,
Fuck me, fuck me, fuck me,
Fuck me hard, she screamed,
As the neighbours banged on the wall,
This was more than I could have dreamed,
With words That could be heard
Right on down the hall,
I never thought she would be this vocal
When she looked so quiet and demure,
Maybe she was only humouring me
Because she was a whore
But as she got louder,
I thought the neighbours were worried about her life,
In fact, the bitch screamed far too loud
I never heard the bleeding wife

Looking Through The Widows
Of My Soul

My past comes back to haunt me when I'm all alone
The haunted souls of yesteryear echo through my home
My heart rips in two but it bleeds no more,
As guilt and shame rack my aching mind
Tears of frustration roll down my cheeks
As peace I cannot find,
I cared for no one when I was younger
Broke spirits hearts and minds
All in my quest for selfishness
And the material things that I could find,
Trampled people underfoot never heard their pleas
Never worried about anyone only my own needs
Wife and children discarded, friends just tossed aside
All of my emotions, withered wilted and died,
Now my heart is aching, and I feel sad and all alone,
Diary always empty no numbers on my phone,
All this wealth that I have amassed means
nothing anymore
The only love I can find is from an expensive whore,
So I have made my mind up I will take the easy way out,
Go out with a whimper as I seem to of run out of shout
I put my affairs in order go upstairs and run my bath,
Get myself a razor and listen to my demons laugh.

Don't Rush Back

Oh! Well, that's it, the last ones gone,
I don't know whether burst into tears,
Or break into song
I know that may sound cruel,
But give me a break
There's only so much an old bloke can take
No more arguing, no tantrums and tears,
No more worry or needless fears,
Hey Dad, I'm skint can I borrow some cash
I don't know what's happened to the computer
but I think its crashed
I will miss the kids, but they will visit when able
And now I have room for my new snooker table,
Me and the wife can have some time to ourselves
Don't think we have had that since they were twelve,
A sleep in on Sunday, breakfast in bed,
A good night's sleep for my poor aching head,
We have Christmas and Birthdays and telephone calls
Plenty of time to get with them all I do love my kids
Though that may not be how it seems,
But until we babysit, then sweet, sweet dreams,

Why Me?

Here I am sat in the bar, I am waiting for my giro,

Pondering, on my life, wondering where it will go,

Been out of work for three long years,

Job prospects don't look to bright

So, I get out my phone take a gander,

Put on my bets for tonight,

Get myself another pint then I text the wife

Make sure she's got my fillet steak for tea

And sent her a couple of kisses

I think i will watch the match tonight

On my 60-inch plasma screen Its in H.D looks amazing

And the colours are crisp and clean

One of my mates comes in and I sell him some pot

Just something I do on the side, I

Know it's not strictly legal but I hate being skint

Well, I do have my pride,

After a couple of more pints let's phone a cab

This place is shit there's no one here and a little bit drab

I hate getting taxis they stink off piss

Should have brought the Merc

One thing i don't do is drink and drive

What do you think I am some sort of berk?

All About My Love For You

Let me take you for a glass of wine and we
will talk about your eyes
Sometimes I wonder at your beauty but in
reality, I am not surprised
I love everything about you Especially your mind,
You are thoughtful and generous, not forgetting kind
I like the way you think of others,
always put yourself last,
The way you always look to the future
Never dwell on the past
I like to spend time with you So we
can talk like lovers do
If i had to choose between you and a thousand women
You would always be my choice,
By the time you have read this poem
I hope your nice and moist

It's a funny ole World
My wife is always telling me not to have another beer,
So, I always have one, although i quake with fear,
I ain't saying she's formidable, well actually I am,
But for some reason I like to defy her
though it gets me in a jam,
You're not going out with the lads she
says as I put on my coat,
I ain't sitting here on my own as you ram
beer down your throat

I mention for her to come with me,
But if she said yes, I think I would die,
We would only end up fighting,
And she would punch me in the eye,
Because I am not really going with the lads
I got myself a bird,
She has a little bedsit on the corner of fifth and third
Now when we got married she gave me a golden rule,
Not to ever stray or I would lose my bits to a rusty tool,
I knew she wasn't lying and that she meant every word,
But after ten years of her nagging I never really cared
Well that came to haunt when I woke
up screaming with pain,
Blood all over the bed sheets, my life
would never be the same
Now the missus is in Broadmoor, there for life I hope
They did try to stitch it back on,
But it was just a bloody joke
So now I'm missing my Johnston
And I dress up as a girl,
Taking lots of hormones,
My its funny ole world

My Muse

My muse is like an octopus it has so many arms,
Also like a gypsy because it has so many charms
Maybe like a ghost because it haunts my soul,
Or a striker from a football team helps me score a goal
I suppose my muse has many faces
and pulls me many ways,
Like any other muse, sometimes I have bad days
But when my muse is flowing i feel like I can fly
Reach up through those clouds touch a clear blue sky
Sometimes i can sit in front of my
laptop for hours at a time,
Sat there scratching my head and my
balls not even get a rhyme
Then one day i'll sit my arse down and
the words flow thick and fast,
So you write till your fingers ache
Because you don't know how long it will last
Where do I get my muse from, well
it comes from all around
Every tree, every child every little sound
Every time I hear a song my muse it starts to mutter
And every pretty girl I see well then it starts to flutter,
So you have your answer my muse is in my blood,
It's up to other people to say if I'm any good

The Dream Poem

My minds full of ideas that I haven't thought of yet,
And my heart resembles a full moon,
My mouth just wants to eat alphabet noodles,
And I'm a character in a Disney cartoon,
With two big ears and a face full of whiskers,
In my mind I carry a gun,
Don't stand and point if I'm coming your way
Take my advice and run
I like to go swimming in sky blue pink soup,
Wearing a nappy and red swimming cap,
I get chased by a shark in a snorkel and mask,
And I'm worried he gives me the clap,
My house is a mansion but there is so little room,
Don't think that I could swing a cat,
There's a pile of wood in middle of the floor
I wonder if that's where I sat,
A Zebra or elephant I can't really tell
Asks if I want me a nice cup of char,
He brings it out on a tray of carrots and gold,
Then makes me sup out a jar,
I think now i should wake up cos it's all getting strange,
A rabbit is eating my knees,
And when i go to bed tomorrow night,
Can I please have a much better dream.

Living In The Dark

It's amazing how people can be so unkind,
They think you are deaf just because you are blind
They don't mean to be hurtful, but say hurtful things,
Not knowing a casual remark and the hurt it brings,
Because you are blind, they think you can't see,
They are so narrow-minded and that's all they will be,
You see with your ears and see with your touch,
You see through your family that love you so much,
No, it's not easy in a life that never has light,
It's always a struggle and always a fight,
But life has a way and will always win through,
Just hope and pray it never happens to you.

Fireman Sam

I once met a fella while, on a train,

He told me he was a fireman he made that quite plain.

I said you do a good job but don't get much pay,

He replied hey that's life, things just go that way,

How long you been doing it I politely inquired,

Twenty five years i'll soon be retired,

So i bought him a beer, and we continued to chat

About nothing really just this and that

I said do you get a good pension, it's not bad he replied,

It's such a dangerous job did you do it

to conquer fire and learn

He said no I do the job because, I like to

watch things burn.

Love Is

Love is saying you'll climb Mount Everest for her Without any
crampons,
Or going to a packed supermarket to
buy anew pack of tampons,
Returning the favour when she goes on bended knees,
Buying lots of chocolates and always saying please
Love is love letting her win an argument,
When you know that you are right
Telling her you love her each and every night,
Not telling her she smells When
she comes out of the loo,
Love looking in her eyes and saying,
There will never be anyone but you,
Love is giving her the lie in, Early Sunday morning
Not waking her when getting up for
work Just as day is dawning,
But most of all its just being there for her,
Letting her know you love her and that
you will always be there

Oh! To Live In Blighty

Oh! To live in Blighty Where the Summer lasts a day,
The Podophiles are protected So the
kids have nowhere to play,
We have sold off all our Commodities ,
So we pay for everything through our teeth,
Where the Courts send you on holiday
If you decide to become a thief,
Now I don't mean to sound bitter,
But I think i have a point,
When you read a mugger robbed a pensioner.
Because he needed money for a joint,
The Health Service costs a fortune ,
Unless you're a visitor from abroad ,
And the bottom fell out the market,
If I was a banker I'd fall on my sword
The police have been hit by cutbacks,
So every one's at risk
And all the schools are closing
Not a thought about the kids,
Oh to live in Blighty A lovely place is this
No, I'm not being serious,
In fact, I'm taking the piss.

Obsession

I know you don't want to see me,
But honest I just want to talk,
If you still feel the same when i've finished,
I promise, i'll, turn round and i'll walk,
I'm so sorry about how I hurt you,
It was just sex it meant nothing at all,
I was drunk and it was just a quickie,
A knee trembler against the pub wall,
So please say that you'll forgive me,
Because I love you with all my heart,
Let's just put this behind us,
Try again and make a new start,
Why are you being so negative,
You can't forget all that we had,
I know that we had some hard times,
But you have to admit they Were' not all that bad
How can you say I'm controlling?
I only did what i thought best,

Well I suppose that's it then
No way I can change your mind,
Why did I think I could change you?
God I most of been blind,
No, I am not getting angry,
I am getting frustrated again,
How can you say that it's over?
How can you cause me so much pain?

Yes, I will go in a minute,
You know I'm a reasonable man,
But you know if I can't have you,
I will make sure that no one else can.

Widow Edna

Edna has worked her for years now
I suppose since the dawn of time
I see her each day when she's packing ,
And she's still the best girl on the line
Said Edna you're gone sixty-eight now
Have you thought about, well, to maybe retire,
She said i ain't the kind of lady,
Who will spend her days with a
blanket in front of the fire,
I had been with my bill for a long time
And he was my schoolgirl crush,
I miss him and want to see him,
But to be honest, I'm not in that much of a rush,
My kids come and see me quite often,
But their busy and have their own lives ,
They come to visit quite frequently
Ringing my Grandchildren and their Wives,
So i am happy just biding my time here,
Let's be honest what else will I do
But I am in the mood for a
Toyboy and if you're lucky it could be you

Lovers Lane

The night was still the moon was full,
As we drove to lover's lane,
We both knew what was on the menu,
I was hyped like a runaway train,
You were' not the first i had brought here,
You were the last in a very long line,
But things were getting hairy now,
You're going to be the last for quite time, I
Parked up turned out the lights,
And we made small talk for a while,
I said shall we get in the back seat
You gave me a knowing smile,
We got in and started smooching,
Then you removed your top,
I brought out some ribbons
Would you mind if I tied you up?
She said I'm open-minded
But i think enough is enough,
I gave her a slap and said now will you do as i say,
Crying and trembling she nodded,
I smirked and said i always get my way,
I slapped her again, ripped off her clothes,
Then went to get my knifes,
Every one's got their hobbies,

Mine is taking lives,

She looked into my eyes,
Realized that she would never grow old,
A certain bravado took over her,

She suddenly became quite bold,
Why are you doing this you perv,
What have I done to you?
Well she asked, so she deserved an answer
It was the least I could do,
You didn't' I am sorry to say,
To be honest you just caught my eye,
Now just lay back and enjoy it,
Believe me the time going to fly,
Knowing now her fate was sealed
She went for one more throw of the dice
She begged and pleaded offered me money,
Said she would pay any price
Then she said I will do anything,
Get your knob out I will even suck that,
So, I gave her my smile and my maniacs laugh,
And said now where's the fun in that.

Show Me The Money

The hotel room is booked the waitress set,
We are just waiting for you to arrive,
And the things that i have planned for the evening
Just makes me feel so alive the tables laid,
The mood is set the wine is left to breathe,
You look stunning as you walk in the room,
My chest just starts to heave,
Trying to hide my palpitations, and the
quickening of my heart,
I take your coat fetch a bottle of wine,
Then we both make a start,
We started off with some small talk
A little chat about this and that,
The waitress brings the pate,
And a bottle Brut champagne,
I knew we had a little more time
I said let's lighten the mood a little

I brought out some blow
So, we smoked it and the girls got giggly,
I said let's put the main on hold for a while,
Let's move on into the bedroom,
And the girls gave an all-knowing smile,
So off we moved into the bedroom,
And here i am thinking quite clearly,
It's going to be a great night is this
Now I was going give you the details,

And tell you about our fantastic lay,
But alas I overspent on my budget,
And the girls both wanted their money upfront
Alasi could not pay,

Love At first Sight

I met her in a bar i knew I'd fallen in love,
She was oh so beautiful fit me like a glove
We talked for absolutely ages,
Then I asked her back to my flat s
He said I want to powder my nose,
I said i'll grab my hat,
My head was positively spinning,
I was about to get myself laid,
Last time i got my leg over
Iam ashamed to say I paid,
But it seemed those days were over,
Looks like my luck had changed,
She said shall we get a taxi,
I said that can be arranged,
finally we got there,
I tried my hardest not to limp,
I really wanted to impress her,
Not look like a useless gimp,
I got us a drink, and we got comfy,
Then we started to kiss,
My hands they started to wander,
I cupped my hands around her tit,
She never tried to stop me,
You're in boy this is it
A night of unbridled passion,
A night of lustful sin,
I ran my hands up her leg,
Moved it to her thigh

Moved it even higher
And got a big surprise,
When i asked if she had any secrets,
Apparently, she lied,
Had I been more careful
Watched what made her tick,
Because when I went looking for a muff ball
Unfortunately, I. Grabbed a prick

Down With Women's Lib

The women are uprising, time to make a stand,

Now their wanting equal rights, it's getting out of hand

Tie them to the kitchen sink chain them to the bed,

It's about to get nasty, something must be said,

Look at that Emily Pankhurst, chaining
herself to the rails

For gods' sakes cut her down, put her in the jails

Now they say they want to vote, for Christ equal pay

Send them all to Australia, send them on their way

Now it's not that I'm insensitive because
I'm a man of the world

But come on let's be honest, after all they are only girls

Just Another Household

It's well past one and Pete is still not home,
Sandra is so nervous as she waits by the phone,
They have been married so long now
T seems like it's forever,
He never says he loves her,
Always trying to be clever,
He hopes when he gets in,
He won't be too pissed,
Better still she hopes he stays out,
He surely won't be missed,
The kids are asleep she hopes he won't wake them,
Cos if they do, she knows he will hurt them
With his dead lifeless eyes   totally devoid of love,
And his fists of steel that he reigns down from above,
His loveless eyes scare her deep down to her soul,
And his iron fists he uses to keep her under control,
With a shiver and a shudder,
She hears the key in the door,
She hopes he is in a good mood,
Or he will give her what for,
She soon gets her answer, when he turns and snarls,
What you still doing up u checking on me Darls,
No, no she cried trying hard not to whine,
"Wanted to do you something to eat
don't care about the time,"
"Don't talk to me about food look at the state of this floor
What you bin doing all day, you stupid whore,"
"I'm sorry I'm sorry i'll clear it up now, "

It's too fucking late now you stupid cow",

Pete reaches down and grabs Sandra's hair

Get into the kitchen go on get in there,

He pulls her hair out in clumps as he drags her round,

Sandra starts crying as he throws
her down to the ground

Pete pummels her with punches as
Sandra curls up a ball,

Pete only stops when he hears the kids crying in the hall

Seeing her chance, she kicks Pete in the balls,

Clutching his nuts, he groans then he falls,

Sandra stands up and grabs a knife from the rack,

Grasping it with both hands she stabs it deep in his back,

Thinking of freedom, she stabs again and again,

Never again will he hit them or cause them pain,

O, Peter gone to hell in a handcart,

And Sandra's gone to jail,

The kids are in a foster home

Cos the courts won't give mum bail,

Social services have hit the headlines'

Cos they refuse to take the blame,

There's no moral to this story well what can you do,

I suppose just be thankful, it won't happen to you.........

Made in the USA
Monee, IL
31 August 2021

76949661R00059